Look for the Helpers

Adapted by Alexandra Cassel
Based on the screenplays
"A Storm in the Neighborhood" written by Becky Friedman
and "After the Neighborhood Storm" written by Angela C. Santomero
Poses and layouts by Jason Fruchter

Simon Spotlight
New York   London   Toronto   Sydney   New Delhi

"When I was a boy and I would see scary things in the news, my mother would say to me, 'Look for the helpers. You will always find people who are helping.' To this day, especially in times of 'disaster,' I remember my mother's words and I am always comforted by realizing that there are still so many helpers—so many caring people in this world."
—Mister Rogers

SIMON SPOTLIGHT

An imprint of Simon & Schuster Children's Publishing Division
1230 Avenue of the Americas, New York, New York 10020
This Simon Spotlight paperback edition August 2018
© 2018 The Fred Rogers Company
For information about special discounts for bulk purchases, please contact Simon & Schuster Special Sales
at 1-866-506-1949 or business@simonandschuster.com.
Manufactured in the United States of America 0818 LAK
10 9 8 7 6 5 4 3
ISBN 978-1-5344-2629-0
ISBN 978-1-5344-2630-6 (eBook)

Daniel Tiger was with Dad Tiger when he saw dark clouds filling the sky.

"There is a big storm coming to the neighborhood," Daniel said.

"That's right," Dad said. "Our friends are coming to our house so they have a safe place to stay during the storm. It's part of our safety plan."

Soon the sky became even darker. The rain went *whoosh* and the loud thunder went *boom*.

"I don't like storms," Daniel said.

Daniel felt worried.

Mom and Dad told Daniel, "Grown-ups are here to keep you safe."
Then they sang, 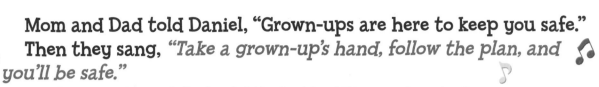 *"Take a grown-up's hand, follow the plan, and you'll be safe."*

That made Daniel feel a little better! He wanted to know more about the plan.

"The first part of our plan," Dad said, "is to find a safe place inside." Daniel felt much better now. His home was a safe place, so they went inside.

Katerina Kittycat, O the Owl, and their families needed a safe place for the storm too. They came to Daniel's house for a family sleepover!

Daniel wished it was sunny so they could play outside.
"Do you want to make believe with me?" Daniel asked his friends.
"Let's make believe that we're playing outside in all kinds of weather."

So many seasons, so many ways to play.

In the springtime, there are raindrops and puddles to splash in.

In the fall, I can play all around in the leaves.

In the winter, build a snowman and make a snow angel.

Swim in the sunshine, enjoy the summer heat!

"What's the next part of our safety plan?" Daniel asked.

Mom said the next step was to make sure they had an emergency supply kit.

Daniel found a flashlight, a first aid kit, and water.

Then all of a sudden, the lights went out!

"Who turned off the lights?" Daniel asked.

"Sometimes a big storm can make the lights go out," Dad said. "But we're right here and you are safe."

Daniel sang, *"Take a grown-up's hand, follow the plan, and you'll be safe."*

Even though the lights went out, Daniel and his friends still had dinner. Dad lit candles and made sandwiches for a grr-ific inside picnic!

Soon, it was time for bed. Katerina and O slept in sleeping bags in Daniel's bedroom!

"I like having everyone around," Daniel said. "It makes me feel safe."

Having a safe place to sleep was the last part of the emergency plan.

In the morning, the rain stopped. The storm was over. Daniel looked out the window and saw tree branches and leaves on the ground. The storm had made a big mess.

Dad Tiger said, "When I was young and I would see scary things, my mother would say to me, 'Look for the helpers. You will always find people who are helping.'"

Later that day, it was safe for Katerina Kittycat, O the Owl, and their families to go back to their tree house.

When Trolley had to stop in the road because of branches on the ground, Daniel was scared. Then he looked for the helpers.

Look for the helpers. Who do you see?

Daniel saw Mr. McFeely. He was helping pick up branches. "Thank you for helping, Mr. McFeely!" Daniel said.

The Tiger family went all around the neighborhood to make sure their other neighbors were safe too.

Look for the helpers. Who do you see at the castle?

Prince Wednesday and his family were helping by cleaning up.

Look for the helpers.
Who do you see at the Museum-Go-Round?

Miss Elaina and her mom were helping clean up the neighborhood too!

When Trolley reached the Clock Factory, Daniel and his family saw that a big tree had fallen down in front of it. Daniel was scared. Then he remembered the song. He sang, *"Take a grown-up's hand, ♪ follow the plan, and you'll be safe."* ♪

He reached for his dad's hand. Then he looked for the helpers.

Even Trolley was a helper! Trolley pulled the tree away from the Clock Factory.

Daniel was a helper too. He planted a new tree to help everyone remember how they helped the neighborhood after the big storm.

The big storm was a little scary, but Daniel felt better when he looked for the helpers. There were a lot of helpers! Ugga Mugga!

Do you want to learn more about staying safe and about looking for helpers? Read on for some helpful advice from Daniel Tiger and friends!

Staying Safe Every Day

Even when there isn't an emergency, you can stay safe every day by wearing a seat belt, staying with a trusted grown-up, wearing a helmet, and more. Can you think of other things you can do to stay safe?

Staying Safe in an Emergency

Emergencies can be scary because they sometimes happen very suddenly, but there are things you can do before, during, and after an emergency to stay safe. Turn the page to learn more. . . .

BEFORE AN EMERGENCY

Make a Safety Plan:

Daniel Tiger's family has a safety plan to help them prepare for the storm. Ask your parent or caregiver to make a plan too, before a storm or other kind of emergency. A good safety plan includes:

A safe place to stay inside
This might be your home, or it might be a friend's or relative's house.

An emergency supply kit
You'll find suggestions for what to include in an emergency kit on the next page!

Canned and dry food and bottled water
If the power goes out, you will need food on hand that doesn't need to be refrigerated to stay fresh. You'll also want to eat any fresh food right away before it goes bad and have lots of bottled water to drink. Look for more suggestions on the next page.

A safe place to sleep and a routine
Whenever possible, try to stick to a routine. For example, once you are in a safe place, try to go to bed at the same time as usual.

Make an Emergency Supply Kit:

Parents and caregivers: Here is a list of some things you might want to include in an emergency supply kit for a storm or other kind of emergency:

Food and water

Canned and dry food (and a can opener) and bottled water (at least one gallon of water per person per day).

First aid kit

Include things like adhesive bandages, antibiotic ointment, and more. Also consider having any medicine you or your family might need, stored in child-proof containers.

Flashlights, batteries, and more

Make sure to have flashlights, extra batteries, and a battery-powered or hand-crank radio. If you have a cell phone, be sure to bring a charging cord.

Hygiene

Toothbrushes, toothpaste, and soap.

Clothing and blankets

Warm blankets, extra clothing, and sturdy shoes.

Entertainment

Books and games can help pass the time, and a child's favorite stuffed animal or toy can be comforting.

DURING AN EMERGENCY

Here are some things you can do if you get worried during an emergency:

- Take a deep breath.
- Listen, watch, and follow instructions.
- Hold on to a grown-up's hand. It's important to stay with a helper who will keep you safe.

AFTER AN EMERGENCY

After an emergency, things might not be the way they used to be. It can take some time to get used to these changes. Here are some ways you can start to feel better:

- Use your words to describe how you are feeling. Are you scared, sad, angry, or lonely? You can also draw a picture that shows how you are feeling.
- If you are confused, ask questions. A grown-up will help you understand what happened during the emergency.
- Keep a routine, like brushing your teeth after breakfast or singing a song before bed. Even if many things feel different, some things can stay the same.

Look for the Helpers in Your Neighborhood:

Another thing you can do after an emergency is to look for the helpers. Every day, there are grown-ups who help keep you safe. Here are some people who can help with an emergency:

Your Parents or Caregivers

They can help keep you safe at home.

Doctors or Nurses

They can help you if you are hurt.

Firefighters

They can help put out fires and help clear dangerous objects from roads.

Teachers

They can help keep you safe when you are at school.

"Look for the Helpers" Song:

Daniel sings this song if something scary happens. You can sing this song too, and remember to look for the helpers.

When things seem bad or scary,
just take a look around.
You'll see that people help each other.
People help all over town.

Look for the helpers.
Look for the helpers.

Doctors, nurses, firefighters,
and policemen, too.
They'll help you out and keep you safe.
They're here to help you.

If you are scared or frightened,
just look around and see
that people always help each other.
People help those in need.

Look for the helpers.
Look for the helpers.